WITHDRAWN

THIS WALKER BOOK BELONGS TO:

_____

_____

_____

School's Service

To Jeanette Larson

First published 2003 by Walker Books Ltd
87 Vauxhall Walk, London SE11 5HJ

This edition published 2004

2 4 6 8 10 9 7 5 3 1

This book has been typeset in Veronan

Printed in Italy

British Library Cataloguing in Publication Data:
a catalogue record for this book is available from the British Library

ISBN 0-7445-9832-X

www.walkerbooks.co.uk

WALKER BOOKS
AND SUBSIDIARIES

LONDON · BOSTON · SYDNEY · AUCKLAND

FELIX

AND THE WORRIER

ROSEMARY WELLS

Felix's mummy
buttoned Felix
into his pyjamas and
told him his story.

She gave Felix his Mitey-Vite
and made sure all his animals
were under the covers.
Felix floated into Dreamland
on clouds of happiness.

But when all the world
lay fast asleep,
someone tapped on
Felix's window.
It was the Worrier.

The Worrier hopped right in
and sat down.
"I'm worried about that
little black spot
on your tooth," he said.

Felix's clouds of happiness
disappeared.

Felix and the Worrier worried about
the little black spot on Felix's tooth
until the morning sun rose in the sky.

"Bye-bye!" said the Worrier.

Before breakfast
Felix told his mummy
about the
little black spot.

Felix's mummy looked very carefully.
"Every tooth is as white as snow,"
she said. "My little buttercup, you
have worried for nothing."

Felix did not see the Worrier all day.

At bedtime Felix
drank his Mitey-Vite.
"Tomorrow is the playschool
picnic in the park!" said Felix's mummy.
"It will be such fun!"
But in the middle of the night ...

Tap, tap, tap!

"Don't forget," whispered the Worrier.
"Bruno and the big boys
want to pull your trousers off and
throw them in a tree!"
Felix worried about Bruno
and the big boys all night long.

On the way to the park, Felix told his mummy about Bruno and the trousers-in-the-tree threat.

But Bruno and the big boys were nowhere in sight. "You worry too much, my little firefly," said Felix's mummy.

"Tomorrow is your birthday," said Felix's
mummy. "Are you worried about anything?"
"No," said Felix. "I am not worried."
"Really?" asked his mummy.
"Really, really, really!" said Felix.

But in the wee hours, Felix had a visitor.

"Supposing nobody
comes to
your birthday party?"
said the Worrier.

"Supposing you get presents
you don't like?

Toys that do scary things!

Books too hard to read!

Clothes that don't fit!

Anything can happen!"

Suddenly Felix heard a funny noise.

**Bow! Wow!
Wow!**

went the noise.
"That noise worries me!"
said the Worrier.
"I am not going to worry!"
said Felix. "I am going to find out
what that noise is!"

In the kitchen was a
mysterious birthday box.

**Bow! Wow!
Wow!**

said Rufus from inside the box.
Felix opened the box.

"Oh, no!" said the Worrier.
"Dogs worry me more than
anything in the world!"

The Worrier jumped into the night sky
and went to worry somebody else.

Felix and Rufus slept
on clouds of
birthday happiness
together.

WALKER BOOKS is the world's leading
independent publisher of children's books.
Working with the best authors and illustrators
we create books for all ages, from babies
to teenagers – books your child will
grow up with and always remember. So…

FOR THE BEST CHILDREN'S BOOKS,
LOOK FOR THE BEAR